We Came To America is dedicated to all the children who come to America. May they find peace, freedom, and prosperity in their new home. May we welcome them and inspire them to sustain a love and dedication to peace, freedom, and justice for all.

WE CAME TO AMERICA

FAITH RINGGOLD

Alfred A. Knopf   New York

We came to America,
Every color, race, and religion,
From every country in the world.

Some of us were already here
Before the others came.

And some of us were brought in chains,

Losing our freedom and our names.

We came to America,

Every color, race, and religion,
From every country in the world.

We traveled from our birthplace

By boat and by plane.

Some of us came running

From injustice, fear, and pain.

We came to America.

Every color, race, and religion,
From every country in the world.

We brought along our joyful songs,
Our stories wise and true.

Our music colored the air,
Beautiful sounds and patterns everywhere.

Our joyful dance now freed our pain,
Gently, like soothing rain.

Our food, our fashion, and our art
Made America GREAT.

We came to America,

Every color, race, and religion,
From every country in the world.

In spite of where we came from,

Or how or why we came,

We are ALL Americans,

Just the same.

We came to America,
Every color, race, and religion,
From every country in the world.
Some of us were already here
Before the others came.
And some of us were brought in chains,
Losing our freedom and our names.
We came to America,
Every color, race, and religion,
From every country in the world.
We traveled from our birthplace
By boat and by plane.
Some of us came running
From injustice, fear, and pain.
We came to America,
Every color, race, and religion,
From every country in the world.
We brought along our joyful songs,
Our stories wise and true.
Our music colored the air,
Beautiful sounds and patterns everywhere.
Our joyful dance now freed our pain,
Gently, like soothing rain.
Our food, our fashion, and our art
Made America great.
We came to America,
Every color, race, and religion,
From every country in the world.
In spite of where we came from,
Or how or why we came,
We are all Americans,
Just the same.

THIS IS A BORZOI BOOK PUBLISHED BY ALFRED A. KNOPF

Copyright © 2016 by Faith Ringgold

All rights reserved. Published in the United States by Alfred A. Knopf,
an imprint of Random House Children's Books,
a division of Penguin Random House LLC, New York.
Knopf, Borzoi Books, and the colophon are registered trademarks
of Penguin Random House LLC.

Visit us on the Web! randomhousekids.com
Educators and librarians, for a variety of teaching tools,
visit us at RHTeachersLibrarians.com

Library of Congress Cataloging-in-Publication Data
Names: Ringgold, Faith, author, illustrator.
Title: We came to America / Faith Ringgold.
Description: First edition. | Alfred A. Knopf : New York, [2016]
Summary: Celebrates United States immigration and the country's
diverse immigrant heritage.
Identifiers: LCCN 2015035221 | ISBN 978-0-517-70947-4 (trade)
ISBN 978-0-517-70948-1 (lib. bdg.) | ISBN 978-0-553-51257-1 (ebook)
Subjects: | CYAC: Emigration and immigration—Fiction. | Immigrants—Fiction.
United States—Emigration and immigration—Fiction.
Classification: LCC PZ8.3.R4595 We 2016 | DDC [E]—dc23
LC record available at http://lccn.loc.gov/2015035221

MANUFACTURED IN CHINA
May 2016
10 9 8 7 6 5 4 3 2 1
First Edition